CW00841561

Halloween Tales

from the Black Cat

Diana Molly

Snack in the Mystery house

Oh, hi there, pretty little troublemakers! I know you want to read an interesting Halloween story that will make your skin crawl! And as I am the famous Black Cat, I will make sure that you get what you want.

Here is a story about a witch, and how you must be careful to not accidentally bump into one. Enjoy as much as you want. Only don't complain later that the story was scary. You asked for it yourselves! Enjoy, while I go and make myself busy with the glitter I'm not supposed to tell anyone.

Chapter 1. The Halloween Evening

It was the Halloween evening. Mary and her two best friends – Helena and Lucy – were in her house, getting ready to celebrate. The three of them were very beautiful but looked different from each other. Mary had long blond hair and green eyes, Helena had black hair and blue eyes, and Lucy had fiery red hair and brown eyes. Being ten years old, the three best friends loved to go trick-or-treating on Halloween evening.

"I am going to be a witch," Mary announced happily, getting her costume out of her closet. It was a black robe with bright orange belt and a sharp pointed hat, exactly like the witches' hats.

"Wow, Mary, this is so cool!" Helena exclaimed. "You will look like a real witch!"

"Witches have broomsticks to ride on," Lucy said. "Without one you will not look like a real witch."

Mary looked at Lucy, smiling meaningfully. "I have thought of that, too," she said. Then she walked around her bed and bent down. When she straightened up again, she was holding a broomstick with a long handle. The broomstick was brown and seemed to be handmade.

"I made it with my mom yesterday," Mary said proudly. "The whole costume is made by the two of us. This robe is my dad's old bathrobe – my mom made it shorter for me, and I made an orange belt from one of my old t-shirts."

"You are so talented!" Helena said. "The costume is so adorable. And how did you make the hat?"

"To be honest, we haven't made it," Mary said. "My mom has bought it."

"Anyways, it is fun," Lucy said. "And I will be wearing a panda's costume. A bit boring, but my elder sisters took the best outfits, so I was left with this one," she added, taking the clothes out of her bag.

"Don't worry, it's also pretty," Mary said. "Besides, who told you that the Halloween costumes had to be scary? Your cute panda's costume is really nice."

Lucy sighed but didn't say anything.

"And you, Helena?" Mary turned to her other friend. "What are you going to be?"

"Ta-daa!" Helena exclaimed, taking a white sheet out of her bag.

"Wait, what's that?" Mary and Lucy asked together, gaping at the sheet.

"A ghost's costume, of course," Helena said proudly. "I didn't have time to think about what I was going to wear, so I started whining, of course."

The girls giggled.

"Then my brilliant mom came up with the idea of just tossing a white sheet over my head, and I'm ready!"

"Oh, wonderful," Mary said, still giggling. "The quickest decision ever made. And looks convincing, too!"

"Thanks! I'll tell my mom," Helena said happily.

Mary looked at the clock and nodded. It was already evening. She checked her reflection in the mirror and smiled.

The three of them quickly put on their costumes right over their clothes, with Helena just tossing her sheet over her head, then they took their baskets and looked at each other.

"Girls, are you ready?" Mary asked, and they nodded.

"Mom, dad!" Mary called into the living room. "We're going treat-or-treating! We'll be back soon!"

"Have a good time, girls," Mary's mom called back.

"Be careful!" Her father added, and Mary chuckled.

"Haha, as if there's something dangerous waiting for us in our own neighborhood!" She said, tossing her long blond hair over her shoulder and grabbing her broomstick with one hand, while holding her basket in the other.

"Okay, let's go," Helena said and opened the door. The girls followed her out and looked around.

It was twilight, but not dark yet. There was no sun in the sky, but the sun's late rays were still dimly lighting the sky with pink, orange and purple colors. Helena's big blue eyes could be seen from under the large white sheet she was wearing over her head.

"Oh, Helena," Lucy said, "The lamps reflect

the white color of your sheet making you look like a real ghost!"

Helena giggled joyfully. "I know! That's why I chose this outfit. But your panda's is also nice. Looks great with your ginger hair."

"Oh, thanks! And look at Mary! If I didn't know she was our friend, I would have thought she was a real witch."

"I made this broomstick with special care. It looks real, doesn't it?" Mary asked her friends, examining the tip of her broomstick proudly.

Giggling and talking, the girls went trick-or-treating in their big neighborhood. It was fun, and most of the people of the neighborhood loved their outfits. They gave them much candy, and soon the girls' baskets were half-full with chocolates, lollipops and many other sweets.

It was already dark, but there were still many people with kids in the streets, some playing, others trick-or-treating.

Mary was already tired and a bit bored.

"Girls, what do you think we should do now?" She asked her friends. "We went to nearly every house here."

"No, not every," Lucy interrupted. "There are several more houses that way," and she pointed to the opposite direction. The street there seemed abandoned, as nobody went to walk there with their kids. The street lamps were on, but that street seemed a bit scary to them.

Chapter 2. The Strange Big House

The girls stood there, looking at the empty street and the houses standing on the two sides of it.

Helena frowned. "Every time I come home from school, this street seems strange and kind of empty, even in the daylight."

"I've also noticed it," Lucy said. "There aren't many people here. Interesting, why is it like that?"

"Because there aren't many houses here," Mary said confidently. "Just a few. That's why there aren't many people there."

"There aren't *any* people there," Helena corrected her.

"But what does it matter?" Lucy asked.

"We can go and get more candy here, don't you think so?" Mary asked her friends, smiling widely.

Helena and Lucy also smiled, nodding, as they got ready to fill their baskets till the edge.

There were a few kind people living in the houses on that street, and they gave the girls candies.

"There is only one house left on this street," Mary said excitedly. "The biggest one."

Helena and Lucy looked. At the end of the street a big three-storied house was standing. There were no lights on, and it seemed empty. There were a couple of crooked trees standing in front of the house and there were no street lamps near it.

The girls walked towards that house and stopped in front of it. The door was open ajar.

Mary took a few more steps and peeked inside.

"Girls," she whispered, "I can see snacks on the table!"

Helena and Lucy chuckled softly, covering their mouths.

"I think the homeowner has left the snacks on the table especially for those who go trick-or-treating," Helena said.

"Then let's get inside and take them," Lucy said, smiling.

Mary nodded and slowly entered the dark house. Her friends followed her. There really were a few snacks left on the small table in the hallway.

"Wait!" Mary whispered. "Let's look around the house at first to see if there is anyone inside."

"All right, you go and we shall wait here for you," Helena said.

"When we see the homeowner returning, we shall call you so we can quickly run away," Lucy added.

Mary nodded and slowly walked along the hallway. The house was rather big. She was afraid to turn on the light – what if there were people asleep in the house? The hallway turned to the right, and soon Mary became all alone in the dark hallway, leaving her friends behind.

Suddenly she heard hooting. Jumping up with a start, Mary turned around and saw a pair of big round sparkly eyes looking right at her from a very short distance. She almost screamed, but covered her mouth in time – she didn't want her voice to be heard in the house.

In a few seconds Mary realized that it was an owl and let out the breath she was holding.

She reached the backdoor and stopped. There was a big broomstick lying on the floor. But it was so similar to the broomstick she herself was holding! It wasn't a regular broom for swiping the floor. It was like a real witch's broomstick.

Shrugging, Mary looked around. She was in the kitchen. There were big and small cauldrons lined up on the floor against the wall and a big box full of small carrots. When she kneeled and looked closely at the carrots, she realized that they weren't carrots – they were fingers!

Screaming, Mary ran out of the kitchen and started running down the hallway. It was dark, and she got confused where the entrance was.

"Helena! Lucy! Where are you?" Mary called them, breathlessly running here and there. No response came. "I saw a broomstick and an owl! Cauldrons and strange fingers! This is the house of a witch! Don't touch anything! We must run away from here!" She kept shouting, but her friends didn't make a sound. There was silence; only a couple of cats were meowing somewhere.

"Helena! Lucy!" Mary called desperately. The owl began hooting again, making Mary jump up. At last she found her way to the main door and stopped by the hallway table. Helena and Lucy weren't there. Mary looked at the table and saw that the snacks were gone.

Chapter 3. The Strange Black Cats

"Oh, no! You ate the snacks and ran away!" Mary shouted angrily and reached for the door to run after her friends, when something soft touched her feet. Mary gasped and looked down: it was a black cat. The second black cat came to her too, looking up at her meowing loudly.

"Oh, so the witch also has cats! Black cats!" Mary screamed and dropped her basket onto the floor. She turned back and started running in the opposite direction. The cats meowed even louder and ran after her. Terrified, Mary ran and ran until she reached a wall and stopped. The two black cats came and stood in front of her, meowing loudly and looking at her with their sparkling eyes. One of the cats had blue eyes, and the other cat had a few hairs that were red.

"Please stop meowing, cats!" Mary asked them. "The witch will hear your voices from wherever she is now and will return! I don't want her to see me in her house! Let me get out of the house!"

But the cats didn't give way to her. Instead,

they meowed more loudly.

"My friends have left me here and run away," she said. "Please let me go, too."

One of the cats turned its head from side to side so fast, that it seemed to Mary that the cat was shaking its head.

"What? You don't agree with me?" Mary asked the cat. The cat shook its head again, jumping up and down gladly.

"Wait a minute," Mary said, looking at the cats with interest. "You have blue eyes, and this other cat has got a tassel of ginger hair… could it be…? Helena? Lucy?" Mary whispered, looking at the cats. Both cats started nodding happily and meowing loudly, as Mary stared at them with open mouth.

Mary realized that the cats were Helena and Lucy. Somehow that had managed to turn into cats, but how exactly, Mary didn't know. Anyways, she had to turn them back into humans otherwise they would not be able to go home. Or, even if they went home, their parents would be terrified.

"Helena, Lucy, this is a witch's house!" Mary whispered, not knowing what else to say to the cats that were staring at her. "Did you eat the snacks?" She asked the cats.

They started nodding.

"Oh, I see now," Mary said. "Now I understand! You ate the snacks and turned into cats, because the snacks were magical!"

The cats nodded again, this time very sadly. At that moment the owl hooted again, and the three of them jumped up.

"Girls, what can we do to turn you back into humans?" Mary asked, not knowing the response. "What if the witch will return home now and will find us here?" She shivered. "I don't even want to think about what she will do if she finds out we have entered her house without permission!"

The cats were silent. Suddenly the blue-eyed cat, Helena apparently, ran towards the kitchen. Lucy followed her.

"Girls, where are you going?" Mary called and ran after them. She had to turn on the light in the kitchen to see the cats, because it was very dark there already. The cauldrons and the box full of fingers were still on the floor against the wall, which made her shudder. The black cat that was

Helena was trying to open the lowest drawers of the kitchen cabinet, while Lucy was sniffing the fingers with a terrified expression on her face.

Mary saw Helena opening a few drawers, not understanding anything. Then she saw a copy-book in one of the drawers.

"The recipe-book!" She exclaimed, running towards the cat and taking the copy-book. "Helena, you are a genius! We can make a magical potion to turn you back into human beings!"

Chapter 4. The Potion Recipe

The other black cat came running towards them, to see what Mary and Helena were up to.

Mary opened the copy-book and looked inside. "Oh, good! There are many recipes here. Now I'll try to find the one we need."

The cats were silently watching Mary, as she was trying to read the recipes in the copy-book.

"Animal potion," Mary read the titles. "Horrible potion, Birthday potion, Slumber potion, Laughing potion, Special potion for cleaning the broomstick, Acne potion, Dirty potion, Punishing potion," Mary turned to look at the cats. "Girls, there are so many potions here! The witch will return till I finish reading!"

The cats didn't make a sound. Mary sighed and continued reading. "Vanishing potion, Invisible potion, Blood potion, Tear potion, Hungry potion, Angry potion, Dummy potion, Beauty potion, Elixir of immortality, Dry potion, Dangerous potion, Difficult potion (never tried), Anti-magic potion," Mary read and stopped, gasping. "Girls! I think I've found what's needed for us."

The cats' eyes glowed with happiness.

"Now I'll read the instructions," Mary said excitedly. "*Put three human fingers and three tassels of adercorn hair in the cauldron and add a cup of water. Put on the fire and mix with a wooden spoon until the mixture starts simmering. Then put in two shells, three slices of potato skin and mix vigorously. Add a little Miniscili Powder. The mixture will turn bright blue. It will undo the latest magic done to someone.*"

Mary smiled happily. "Girls, this is it. Now I'll make a potion for you. But we need to be very quick. I'm scared to think of the witch coming back."

Mary ran towards the cauldrons and picked one of them. She put it onto the stove and looked around. "I know where to get the fingers, even though the idea of it terrifies me, but I don't know where to get the other ingredients!"

She put three fingers in the cauldron. "I need adercorn hair, shells, potato skin and Miniscili Powder."

Mary started rummaging in the drawers and

cupboards. She screamed with happiness when she found the potatoes and shells, but she still needed to find the adercorn hair.

The two cats were also looking for the ingredients, trying to help Mary. Helena jumped onto the cupboard and opened the topmost drawer. The adercorn hair was there. It was put there in a big pack, tied with a thread. The adercorn hair was yellow. Mary saw and read the little note that was attached on it: *'Adercorn hair. Best for potions.'*

"Great!" Mary exclaimed happily and separated three small tassels from the pack, adding them to the human fingers. "Now it's time to add the water," she said, taking a cup and opening the tap. She poured the water into the cauldron and turned on the stove. Finding the wooden spoon wasn't a problem, as the spoons were in the drawer. She started mixing the potion standing by the stove. Mary looked like a real witch: in her witch's costume, brewing a potion, her broomstick lying on the floor beside her.

"Helena, Lucy, please help me find the Miniscili Powder. Without it the potion will not turn blue," she said. The two cats started to look for the powder, while Mary peeled the potatoes. She added all the ingredients as it was mentioned in the recipe-book, and finally it was time to add the Miniscili

Powder.

"Did you find it, girls?" Mary asked the cats, but they hadn't found yet. Becoming worried, Mary started to look for it herself. It was the only ingredient needed to be added, and they didn't have much time, as the witch would return any minute.

Chapter 5. Meeting the Real Witch

There was a drawer that the girls hadn't opened yet. Mary opened it and almost screamed: the Miniscili Powder was there. Hurrying, she took some and dropped into the boiling mixture. The potion immediately turned bright blue and started to emit sparkles. The aroma coming from it was horrible – it smelled like rotten food.

"I'm sorry, Helena, Lucy, but you have to drink this," Mary said, pouring the potion into two cups and putting the cauldron into the sink.

The two cats sniffed the potion and jumped back a few steps, meowing loudly.

"I know, I know, it smells horrible," Mary said, washing the cauldron and putting it in its place. "But it's the best thing we can do now. Otherwise you will be cats for the rest of your lives."

The cats looked at each other with horrified eyes. Then Helena came forward slowly.

"I would advise you to close your nose while drinking," Mary said. "But I am not sure how the cats can drink while closing their noses."

Helena looked at Mary and meowed. Mary decided that Helena was giggling. When she had finished cleaning the kitchen and putting everything in its place, she turned to look at her friends. The cats looked more decisive now than before, so Mary took their cups and brought them close to the cats. Helena closed her eyes and drank it in one gulp, but Lucy looked like she would throw up and didn't even come close to her potion.

Suddenly the cat that was Helena started to change. Lucy and Mary watched as the other cat turned into Helena, holding her white sheet and the basket.

"Great!" Mary exclaimed, hugging her friend. "Lucy, now it's your turn."

The black cat sniffed the potion and closed her eyes. She was determined and disgusted at the same time.

"Come on, Lucy, it's not difficult," Helena was urging her. "I drank it and it's not so disgusting, really," she added. "Perhaps only a little bit, like… like bad lemonade, maybe," she added, not knowing what else to say to convince her friend.

Lucy looked at Helena, rolling her eyes, but came closer to the cup of potion anyways.

"Drink it! Hurry up!" Mary said, looking out of the window and realizing that it was already very dark. "The witch will come any minute, and you will stay that way forever!"

Lucy closed her eyes and drank the potion entirely – apparently Mary's words had terrified her and brought her back to reality.

In a few seconds Lucy was standing in front of them, wearing her panda costume and holding her basket.

"Excellent!" Mary said, straightening her costume and grabbing her broomstick. "Now, let's go!" Mary turned off the light in the kitchen.

The three girls left the kitchen and started walking quickly towards the main door. Mary grabbed her basket, put in some of the candies that had fallen out of it and stretched her hand towards the door to open it.

At that moment the owl hooted loudly and the door opened by itself.

Screaming, the girls jumped back a few steps, shivering. The witch entered.

For a moment no one spoke. Helena was standing in the middle of Mary and Lucy, the white sheet over her head, hoping that the witch wouldn't see her under the sheet. Lucy wished she could turn into a real panda and run away, and Mary stood there, looking exactly like the witch who had just entered – with pointed black hat, black robe and a broomstick in her hand.

The witch looked at the three of them, and then her gaze came to rest upon Mary, making her squirm.

"Are you a witch?" The witch asked her. The witch's voice was very croaky and unpleasant. She was an old woman with long grey hair that was sticking out from under her pointy hat, thin bony hands that were holding her broomstick and long crooked nose.

Mary got surprised from the question. She raised her eyebrows, thinking that the witch was crazy, when suddenly she remembered that she was wearing a witch's costume. Without thinking she blurted out the response.

"Y… yes, I am. I am a witch."

The words sounded so funny, and at the same time put such a big responsibility upon her, that Mary didn't know to laugh or to cry.

The witch continued to look at her. "And these are your strange friends, I see?" She asked Mary.

"Yes, they are," Mary said. "I apologize that we're here… We confused the house. We shall go now."

"I am in need of human fingers," the witch said, blocking their way. "I will only let you and your friends go if you prove that you are a witch."

Mary held her breath. How would she be able to prove that she was a witch if she wasn't?

"I… I…" Mary stammered. Then she remembered. Of course! She could prove that she was a witch. Perhaps it would work, she hoped desperately.

"I can brew Anti-Magic Potion," she said, and her friends gasped.

The witch raised her eyebrows. "You can? How do you make that potion, tell me now."

Mary closed her eyes, trying to remember the names of the ingredients and the way of making the potion.

"Well," she said, trying to sound professional. "For brewing that potion we need three human fingers, three tassels of… of … abercorn hair, two shells, three slices of potato peel and …"

"First of all, not abercorn, but adercorn," the witch said strictly.

"Yes, I meant it," Mary said. "I meant to say adercorn!"

"All right, and what's the last ingredient?" The witch asked her.

Mary had forgotten the name of the last ingredient. She only remembered that it was powder, but what was the name?

"Miniscili…" She heard Helena whispering from under the white sheet.

"What?" The witch asked, thinking that it was Mary who had whispered.

"I was saying Miniscili Powder," Mary said, smiling, too happy that Helena had prompted her.

"Oh, all right, I see, I see," the witch said. "Only a real witch will know that potion, exactly. You can go now. By the way, I like your dress. And your broomstick, too. Is it a fast one?"

"Is it a … what?" Mary asked her, as she was hurrying towards the door, her friends following her.

"I was saying, is that a fast broomstick? Does it fly fast?" The witch asked.

"Yes, very fast," Mary said, getting out of the house. "Thank you, now we shall go," she added, hurriedly walking away from the house, her friends by her sides. She turned back to look at the witch and happily saw that the door was closed already.

Chapter 6. The Important Lesson

Mary, Helena and Lucy let out their breaths with relief. They were already near their own houses and there was no danger to meet the witch again.

"It's amazing how we got away from the witch! She said she needed fingers!" Helena said in a whisper.

"It didn't seem funny then, but now I laugh at the way you fooled the witch, Mary," Lucy said. "And she really believed you!"

Mary giggled. "I told her the ingredients of the potion, and she believed, because no other person would know it."

"And she liked your costume, too!" Helena said, laughing. "And the broomstick! Imagine her face if you told her that you and your mom had made it the previous evening!"

The girls laughed happily, now that they were safe and away from the witch's house.

"But it really was dangerous," Lucy said.

"We were so foolish to go inside a stranger's house!" Helena said.

"We should have knocked at the door at first, and if nobody opened it, we should have gone away," Mary said. "It was very impolite of us to act like that."

"It was a scary lesson, but at least we know now what we must do in the future," Lucy said.

"Girls, I think it's already time to go home," Mary said. "It's evening, and our parents may worry about us."

"You are right, Mary," Helena and Lucy said. "Good night!"

The girls went to their houses, keeping in mind the life lesson they got that evening and deciding not to make such mistakes again.

Hey, pretty little troublemakers? Did you enjoy the story? I am sure you also learned that it's not a good idea to get into other people's houses without knocking at first. If not, then beware! Make sure you know a couple of potions' recipes, who knows; maybe it will come in handy!

I liked the black cats, though, as they looked like me, even though they were girls in reality.

Anyways, wait for more stories, scary, of course! I'll be waiting for you! Bye!

Lonely vampire and the garlic girl

Oh, hi there, pretty little troublemakers! So you're here for... let me guess – to read a scary story about Halloween, right? Of course! And as I am the famous Black Cat, I will make sure that you get what you want.

So, here is a story about a vampire. Enjoy as much as you want. Only don't complain later that the story was scary. You asked for it yourselves! Enjoy, while I go and make myself busy with the pompoms I'm not supposed to tell anyone.

Chapter 1. The Halloween Dinner Party

Maria heard the doorbell and ran to open the door. She was very excited, as all of her friends were coming to her house for the Halloween party she and her parents had organized. Being an eleven-year-old girl, Maria was allowed to be left alone in the house with Nancy, her sitter, while her parents were having fun with their own friends somewhere else.

Her classmates, as well as neighbors' kids entered the house happily, everyone wearing Halloween costumes. Maria was a girl pirate, with a piece of black cloth over her eye, with a cute pirate dress and a plastic sword hanging by her side. There were vampires, witches, robots, cats and ghosts among her friends. All of them entered the house shrieking and clapping their hands. It was so noisy that no words could be heard.

"Oh, you came!" Maria called, opening the door widely and welcoming her friends. And they were many – about twenty kids. She hugged each and every one of her friends, as they entered together, smiling.

"Maria, we are so happy to be having a party

at your house!" Emilia said happily, straightening her witch's hat.

"Yes, and me, too," Victoria said. "A real party, without parents!" Victoria was wearing a black cat's costume and a cat's mask on her face.

"It will be more fun than going trick-or-treating, I am sure!" Lily said. She was wearing a demon's costume with red horns on her head.

Maria was beaming. All her friends, boys and girls, were happy to be celebrating the Halloween with her, at her place, and she was ready. She and Nancy had been waiting for them for an hour.

When the last kid entered, Maria closed the door, but it seemed to her that there was someone else out there, but hiding behind the wall. She hesitated for a minute, looking attentively, but no one else showed up. Shrugging, she closed the door and went into the dining-room to join her friends.

The table was full of various tasty dishes and salads, as well as candies and cakes. Her parents had taken care of the party to be really good, together with the dishes, so that the kids would not stay hungry.

"After the dinner we can play games," Maria said. "I have prepared X-Box, board games as well as karaoke for those who want to sing and dance."

"Yay! Wonderful!" Her friends screamed.

At last all the kids were seated at the table, glancing hungrily at the delicious dishes.

"Girls, boys, please start eating!" Nancy called to the kids. "Otherwise the hot dishes will cool down soon and will not be as delicious."

Maria nodded and started eating. She loved to eat tasty food, but most of all she loved to eat garlic, because of which she smelled like garlic most of the time. She ate garlic with everything else – salads, hot dishes, even snacks!

"Oh, Maria, you are eating garlic again!" Nick, a slim boy with freckles complained. He was sitting next to Maria and hated the smell of garlic. Nick was wearing a vampire's costume, as were Anna, Sam and Kevin.

"Of course! How else am I going to enjoy my meals?" Maria said, smiling. "I think you don't like garlic because you are wearing that vampire's costume," she added. The other kids giggled.

"Maria, I hope you haven't put garlic into

the dishes as well," Vanessa said. "Otherwise most of us will stay hungry today."

"No, no, I haven't," Maria said, giggling. "But here is a large bowl full of garlic, in case someone else likes it," she added, pointing to the big bowl. Her friends shook their heads in disgust. "As you wish!" She said, chuckling.

Soon everyone forgot about the garlic and started eating their dinner and chatting happily. Nancy was also in the dining room, making sure that everyone was happy and contented.

Maria's eyes fell onto the window, and it seemed to her that someone was watching them from the outside, but the second she looked, that person disappeared. Maria became worried a little. She stopped eating and went towards the window. It was getting dark already, as it was evening, but the sky was still pink. Maria opened the window, got out her head and looked around – even under the window – but there wasn't anyone there.

"Maybe it seemed to me, that's all," she said to herself, closing the window again and coming back to sit in her place.

Chapter 2. The Boy in the Vampire Costume

The kids were full and excited to start playing games. Some were playing with the computer in one of the rooms, some were dancing, and some were playing board games. There was noise in the house, and everywhere Maria went, there were many kids playing excitedly.

That was exactly the way Maria wanted her party to be. Everyone happy and excited. She joined in to play with her friends all the games. She started playing a board game with Vanessa, Nick, Victoria and Emilia in the corner of the living room, where the others were singing karaoke and dancing.

Maria looked at the window instantly, almost instinctively, and surely saw a face behind the window. It was a face of a young boy, about her age, who was looking into the room intently, unaware that Maria had seen him this time. He was watching the kids who were singing, dancing and having fun in the living room.

"Excuse me," Maria said to her friends. "Please you continue playing. I will be back soon."

"Why, where are you going?" Emilia asked her.

"Just to… check something," Maria said and got up. She left the house without notifying anyone else and slowly approached the boy who was still calmly standing behind the living-room window.

Even from far she had noticed that the boy was also wearing a Halloween costume – a vampire costume. He seemed to be her age and looked rather nice.

"Hello," Maria said, getting closer to him. "Why are you looking into the house?"

The boy jumped with a start and turned to look at her. He looked at her intently, but there was coldness in his gaze.

"Who are you?" Maria asked again. "I am Maria."

The boy took a deep breath and instantly frowned.

"Listen, if you stay silent, I will call Nancy," Maria got angry. "You are looking into my house, and you don't even want to tell me your name?"

"What is… what is that smell?" At last the

boy asked; a disgusted and scared look on his face.

"Again the smell!" Maria rolled her eyes. "First them, now you! It is garlic, okay? And there is nothing wrong with it! Now please tell me who you are."

"I am a vampire," the boy said.

Maria giggled. "Well, and I am a pirate," she said. "But what is your name?"

"Benny," the boy said after being silent for several seconds. "That is my name. But you surely aren't a pirate the way that I am a vampire."

"Whatever," Maria said, waving her hand. "But why are you spying on us, Benny?" Maria asked.

"Because it is interesting," Benny said.

"What is interesting?"

"The games, the fun that you and your friends are having," he said, shrugging.

"Oh, I see," Maria said. "And where do you live? I have never seen you in our neighborhood," she asked.

"We have just moved into this neighborhood," Benny answered. He was keeping the distance from Maria all the time, so whenever Maria was coming one step closer, he was walking one step backwards, looking scared and disgusted all the time.

"Do you want to come and join us?" Maria asked him, trying to be nice. "I will introduce you with my friends and you will also have fun today."

"Join you? No, no, thanks, anyways," Benny said, and shook his hands, as if to prove that he didn't want to join the other kids.

"Why? I can see that you also want to have a good time, as you are watching how we do," Maria insisted.

"I can't, Maria, because I will bite everyone," Benny said in a low whisper.

Maria looked at him for a moment, and then started to laugh loudly. She could not control her laughter and needed several minutes to calm down.

"Why are you laughing?" Benny asked her. He apparently did not understand that he had said a funny thing.

"Because it was funny!" Maria said. "I like

your sense of humor!"

"Well, it is not so funny for those whom I bite," Benny said.

"Come on, Benny, I know that you are wearing a vampire's costume, I noticed it, but it doesn't mean you have to be so serious about your costume," Maria said. "See, I am wearing a pirate's costume, but it doesn't mean that I must go and say *'Ahoy, this ship is mine! I will kill anyone who takes the treasure!'* See?"

Benny smiled.

"The thing is, you are not a real pirate, Maria," he said. "But I am a real vampire."

Maria blinked. "I know you are kidding," she said at last. "But it's not funny anymore. Either come in and join us, or go home and stop looking into my house."

"If I come, I will bite everyone, but if you are insisting, then I will come and will have fun," Benny said. "But then don't complain if your friends start becoming vampires, too. You know, when a vampire bites someone, they become vampires, too."

Maria stopped smiling. She looked at him

for a long time, and then suddenly took his hand. It was cold as ice. Maria gasped.

"So... so it is true?" She asked him, raising her eyebrows.

"Yes, it is, but please stay with me," Benny said. "I don't have any friends and I am lonely. I can't have friends, because I will bite them and scare them away."

"Oh, Benny, don't worry, I will not go away," Maria said. "Hey, look, how come you don't bite me? Were you lying all this time?"

"I was not lying! You yourself felt how cold I am, didn't you?" Benny said.

"It could be anything," Maria shrugged. "Maybe it is cold this evening, and you just got cold. It doesn't necessarily mean that you are a vampire."

"I can't come close to you," Benny said. "If I come a step closer to you, my head starts spinning. I think it is because of that garlic's smell!"

Maria stayed silent for a while. She had read in the books that vampires avoided garlic. So it could be true.

"Look, I will help you, only please come with me and stay in the cellar until I call you out, all right?" She said at last.

"What if I get thirsty for blood?" Benny asked uncertainly.

"I don't think you will," Maria said. "Besides, there is nobody in the cellar, so you can't bite anyone."

Nodding, Benny followed Maria into the house and right down the steps into the cellar, where it was dark and cold.

Chapter 3. Maria and the Garlic

Maria closed the cellar door carefully and came to join her friends again.

"Listen, everyone," she called, trying to get everyone's attention. "Please stop playing, stop the noise and listen to me!"

Her friends stopped playing and looked at her.

"What has happened, Maria?" Vanessa asked.

"Have you thought of a new game?" Emilia asked excitedly.

"Well, could be," Maria said. "But the game involves garlic."

"Ew!" Nick said, turning his face away. "Only not garlic again!"

"Nick, it is important!" Maria said. "It is very important! Garlic helps people when vampires want to bite them."

Nick started to laugh, and together with him – Anna and Kevin, who were also wearing vampires' costumes.

"So that is why you eat garlic? To protect yourself from us?" Kevin asked, still laughing.

"You are not real vampires," Maria said. "You have just worn costumes. What I am talking about, is the real vampires who drink human blood."

"Real vampires do not exist," Anna said.

"Oh, yes, they do," Maria said. "And you will soon believe me. All you have to do is to eat a small clove of garlic."

But however she tried to convince her friends, none of them even came close to the garlic. Sighing, Maria left her friends to continue playing and went down to the cellar. But the cellar was empty.

"Benny?" Maria called, looking around, but he was nowhere to be seen. "Maybe he got bored and left the house," Maria said to herself and left the cellar. The first person that she met was Nancy. Her neck was bandaged and she looked strange.

"Nancy? What has happened to your neck?"

Maria asked, trying to touch Nancy's neck, but she jumped a step backwards, looking at her angrily.

"Nothing, it is nothing," she said. "I scratched it somewhere."

Maria looked at her suspiciously. "Nancy, please give me your hand," she said.

"My hand? Why?" Nancy became so scared that she put both of her hands behind her back.

"I want to touch your hand to see if it is cold or not," Maria said with such a serious tone, that Nancy looked at her for a moment.

"Maria, dear, why do you want to check if I am cold or warm?" She asked.

"Because I have a big suspicion that a vampire has just bitten you and you have become a vampire yourself," Maria said, whispering.

Nancy gasped, clapping her hand over her mouth. "So you know?!" She whispered.

"Yes, I know that there is a vampire here, named Benny," Maria said. "I had left him in the cellar as I wanted to return later and help him make friends with my friends, but apparently he ran away from the cellar and found you first."

"Oh, no, Maria, it didn't happen like that," Nancy said. "I went down to the cellar to get more lemonade, and saw him sitting there. I started asking him who he was and what he was doing in the cellar, as I was seeing him for the first time. He told me that he was a vampire. Of course I did not believe and asked him to prove it. Now I see how stupid I have been, because he really proved it," Nancy started giggling sadly.

"Oh, Nancy, why did you go down to the cellar?! It was dangerous! I should have warned you!" Maria exclaimed sadly.

"Don't worry, Maria, I will be fine," Nancy said. "Now, what is more important, you need to go and make sure that Benny doesn't bite your friends, because after biting me he felt bad and ran out of the cellar."

"Oh, my goodness!" Maria exclaimed and ran towards the living-room.

Chapter 4. The Vampires

Reaching the living-room, Maria stopped. There was the following scene in front of her eyes:

Benny was standing in the middle of the room, together with Nick, Anna and Kevin. They seemed to be arguing.

"You say that you are a vampire, but look at us, too," Kevin said. "We are also vampires!"

"And you don't have the right to call us unreal vampires, while calling yourself a 'real vampire'!" Nick said angrily.

"I understand that you love this game that you are playing," Benny said. "But unfortunately it is not a game for me. I am a real vampire – drinking blood and such."

Everyone gasped.

"Don't believe him!" Anna said. "He wants to make him look superior over us. We all can see that you also want to play with us, pretending you are a real vampire. And we would play with you, of course, only if you didn't lie to us."

"At first when you appeared here and announced that you were a real vampire, we thought you wanted to make the games more interesting," Kevin said.

"It was okay, but then you started insisting that we stay away from you or eat garlic!" Nick said in a horrified voice. "Garlic! Can you imagine! If you just played with us, it would be okay, but garlic?!"

"I only wanted to warn you that it was dangerous to play with me if you did not eat garlic, that's why I asked all of you to eat garlic!" Benny announced.

"First Maria, then you," Kevin said. "Offering us garlic all the time! Can't we play without eating garlic?"

"No, because I am a real vampire and may bite you while playing," Benny said.

"Prove that you are a real vampire!" Nick said all of a sudden.

"I will not!" Benny said. "You don't understand, it is very dangerous! What if I prove it by biting your neck?!"

Maria entered the room. "Benny!" She

called. Everyone turned around.

"Maria?" He said, looking sad. "I was really thirsty, I am sorry!"

Her friends were looking at her and Benny, not understanding what they were talking about. Maria and Benny were strange, that's for sure, as they were speaking absurd things. For a moment there was silence, as Maria and Benny were looking at each other.

"But I had asked you to stay there until I returned," Maria said loudly. "Now my baby-sitter is also a vampire because of you, do you know about it?"

Her friends gasped audibly.

"I am really sorry, but I couldn't help it, I was so thirsty! But she asked me to prove it, so I proved it!" Benny said.

"What?!" Vanessa asked. "What did he prove, Maria? That he is a real vampire?"

Maria nodded.

"Hey, wait a minute, but what about us?" Nick continued complaining, not quite understanding what was going on. "We are also real vampires. Look, guys, I know why this boy behaves like this! He wants to win in the best costume competition! But we shall not let him win it, because we have worked really hard for winning it, particularly me!"

Nobody said anything. Apparently everyone was thinking that Benny was saying the truth, especially when Maria didn't say that he was lying or something like that.

Suddenly at that moment Nancy entered the living-room, looking pale. The kids standing nearest to the door shrieked, as the new information was still fresh in their minds.

"Maria… Maria, please make them go! I am getting thirsty!" She panted, making everyone scream and run in every direction.

"Oh, no!" Maria exclaimed. "Oh, Benny, what have you done?!"

But it was too late. Benny was also getting thirsty, and seeing Nancy looking at the kids with greedy eyes, he also started looking at them as if he wanted to bite them.

Everyone ran out of the living-room, shrieking loudly. All of Maria's friends ran upstairs and locked themselves inside her bedroom.

Chapter 5. The Mixture in the Cup

Maria, Benny and Nancy stayed alone in the living-room. Maria sat down onto the couch, with Nancy and Benny following her.

"Listen," Nancy said. "There is something that I have heard from my great-grandmother when I was a little girl."

Maria and Benny looked at her questioningly.

"My great-grandmother told me a story about vampires," Nancy said. "And it was a very interesting story."

"Please tell us that story, Nancy," Benny said.

"She told me that vampires really existed, but of course I never believed her," Nancy said. "She told me all about vampires, so now I know everything."

Maria looked surprised. "Nancy, what do you know about vampires?"

"I know everything, including the ways of making a vampire a human being again," Nancy said.

"A human being?" Benny asked, his eyes starting to sparkle.

"Yes," Nancy said. "Of course I never believed any of those stories, but now, seeing that vampires really exist, I started to think that the rest of the stories were also true."

"That is so interesting, Nancy! Please tell us how to turn the vampires back into human beings!" Maria exclaimed. "Then maybe we shall be able to turn you back into humans!"

Benny was also excited and silently waiting for the story.

"It is really easy, Maria, Benny," Nancy said. "If you give a vampire a mixture of lemonade and garlic in a silver cup and he drinks it up, he will turn into an ordinary person."

"A mixture of lemonade and garlic?" Benny repeated, raising his eyebrows.

Nancy nodded. "Yes, but then don't eat the garlic on the bottom of the cup. We must only drink the lemonade with garlic flavor. I know it sounds horrible, and perhaps tastes more horrible than sounds," she said, chuckling. "But if you want to not be a vampire anymore, then you must drink it."

"Nancy, if it is true, then I will make that mixture with big pleasure," Maria said. "And we have a silver cup, too," she added, getting up. "Nancy, Benny, get ready to become human beings again!"

Benny was excited. He was watching Maria taking a silver cup from the living-room cupboard, pouring lemonade into it and dropping a few cloves of garlic into the lemonade.

Nancy was excited, too. She was smiling, happy that her great-grandmother had told her all about vampires and now the stories were helping them out so much.

"I can't believe I am doing this," Maria said happily, mixing the lemonade with a spoon. "Who will be the first to drink this?" She asked when the mixture was ready.

"I think I will," Nancy said. "Really, it is interesting for me, so I want to start. If everything goes well, then you will also drink, Benny, all right?"

Benny nodded joyfully. He couldn't wait for Nancy to drink the strange lemonade and to turn into a human being.

Nancy drank the lemonade quickly and put the silver cup onto the table. There was silence. Maria and Benny were waiting for changes to happen to Nancy and were holding their breaths. Nancy was sitting with closed eyes. She was smiling. Maria noticed Nancy's pale face blushing, which meant she had become an ordinary person.

"Nancy! It worked!" Maria screamed. Nancy opened her eyes, nodding.

"So my great-grandmother had told me the truth, oh my goodness!" Nancy said happily. "And now, Benny, it is your turn."

Maria made another glass of garlic lemonade in the silver cup and gave it to Benny who was impatient and almost shaking of excitement.

Chapter 6. Vampires Only As Costumes

Benny took the silver cup and started to gulp down the garlic lemonade. He scowled for a second, but continued drinking until there were only a few cloves of garlic left on the bottom of the silver cup.

He put the cup on the table and waited. Nancy and Maria also waited. Suddenly Benny smiled widely. "I can feel heartbeat!" He exclaimed. "I have turned into an ordinary boy! I am a human being!"

Nancy and Maria applauded so loudly that in a few minutes Maria's friends unlocked the bedroom door and tiptoed downstairs to see what they were cheering on so happily.

Maria noticed them and waved. "Get down, come here, guys!" She called. "It is not dangerous anymore! Benny is already a human being and will not bite anyone!"

"Oh, so he really was a vampire?" Nick asked, still not believing.

The others giggled.

"And how did he turn into a human being?" Victoria asked.

"Did she turn back into a human being as well?" Lily asked, pointing to Nancy.

"Of course!" Maria exclaimed. "They drank garlic lemonade."

"Garlic lemonade?" Everyone shouted together.

"Yes, in a silver cup," Nancy said, smiling. She, Maria and Benny were silently laughing as the other kids were looking at one another, trying to understand what it meant.

"Thank you, Nancy and Maria, for helping me," Benny said when the noise had stopped. "Without your help, I would still be a vampire, biting innocent people and making them vampires, too."

"I would love to be a vampire, though, a real vampire," Nick said sadly. "Will I become one if you bite me now?"

"I am afraid not," Benny said. "I am not a vampire anymore. I am just an ordinary boy, just like you. But it is not a good thing to want to be, I am honest," he added. "Being a human being is way more interesting and exciting."

"Our Halloween party was more than a party!" Maria exclaimed. "It involved real vampires, strange recipes and finally friendship! Because in the end all of us became friends with Benny as well, and he is not lonely now. Am I right?"

"Yes!" Everyone called.

"We will gladly be Benny's friends, and we will never forget this extraordinary Halloween celebration!" Vanessa added.

"Good for you, Maria, for eating the garlic," Anna said. "Otherwise you would also get bitten and no one of you would be able to make the garlic lemonade."

"Instead, you would run after us to bite our necks," Kevin added, chuckling.

"It is already getting dark," Nancy said. "Kids, your parents may worry if you stay here longer. Benny, your family may also worry, so it will be better if you bid one another good night and go home."

Maria hugged all of her friends one by one, letting them go. When it was Benny's turn, he said:

"Thank you for everything, Maria. I have many friends now thanks to you, and I am a human being. I will always be thankful to you for being so kind to me."

"Kindness is what builds the world," Maria replied, smiling.

"Good for you, Maria," Nancy said, as the last kid left the house and they stayed alone. "I am really proud of you, and I am sure your parents will be proud of you, too. It was very kind of you."

"I couldn't do otherwise, Nancy," Maria said. "I can't leave a helpless and desperate person to continue being helpless and desperate, that's why I helped him."

Hey, pretty little troublemakers? Did you enjoy the story? I am sure you did. I am sure you also learned that kindness kills the evil. Well, not really kills, but makes it disappear. Makes it evaporate like the smoke coming up the fire.

To be honest, I was hoping that the vampire boy would bite more people, but unfortunately it's not something that I choose.

Anyways, wait for more stories, scary, of course! I'll be waiting for you! Bye!

Printed in Great Britain
by Amazon